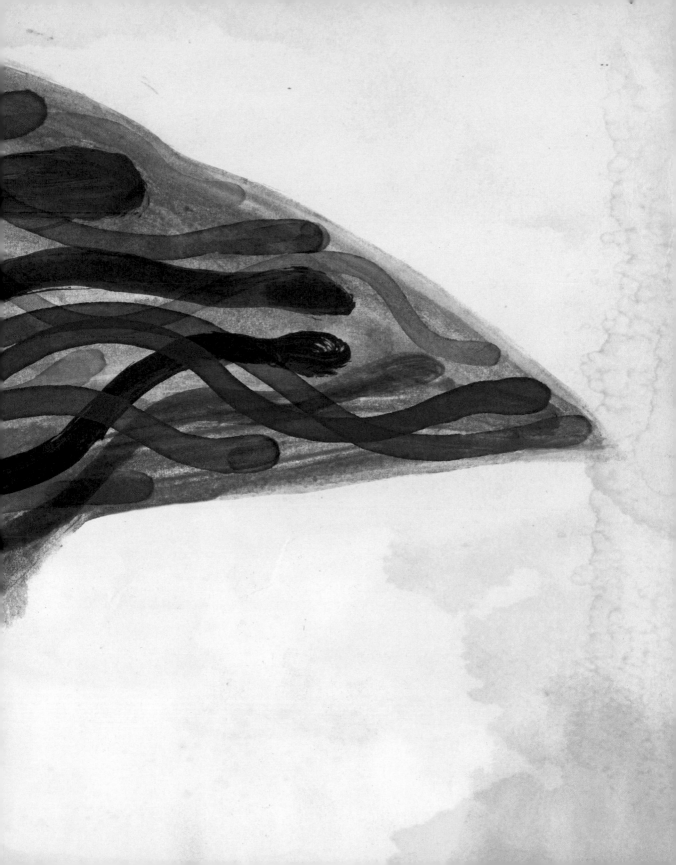

WAR SPREADS THROUGH THE DAY LIKE A WHISPERED, SWIFT DISEASE.

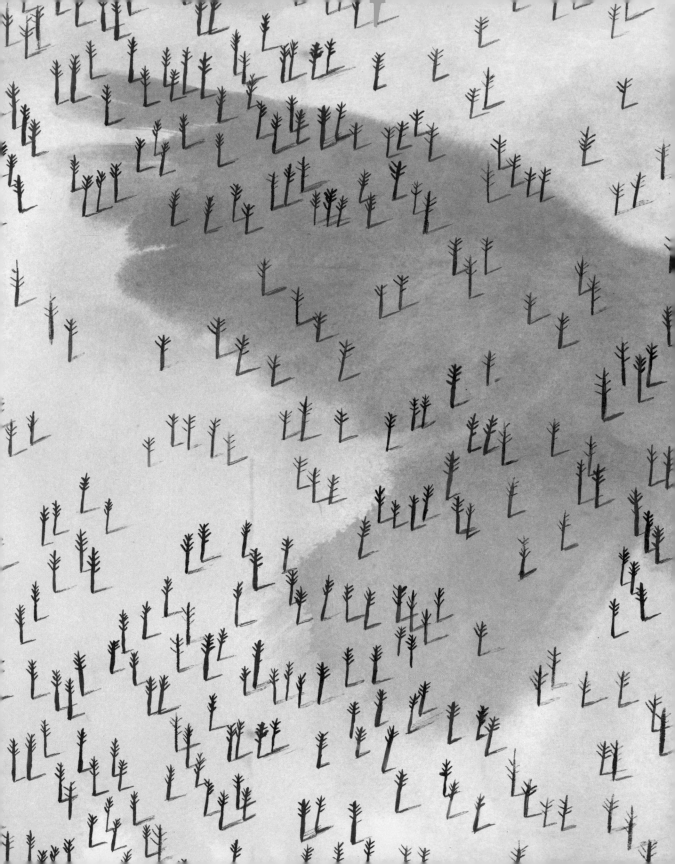

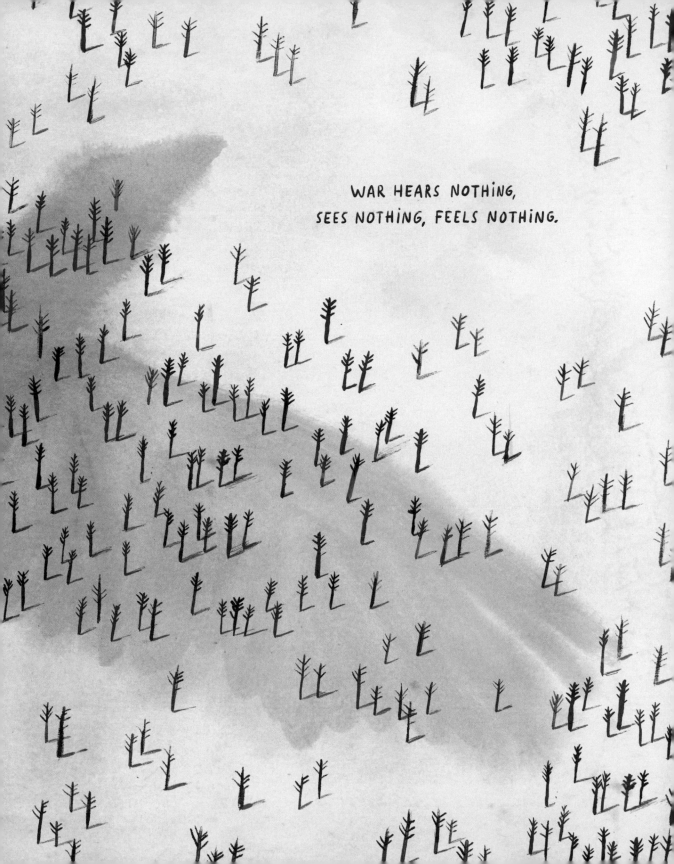

WAR HEARS NOTHING,
SEES NOTHING, FEELS NOTHING.

WAR KNOWS WHERE IT IS FEARED AND WHERE IT IS WISHED FOR.

WAR TAKES ON THE BRUTAL SHAPE OF ALL OUR FEARS.

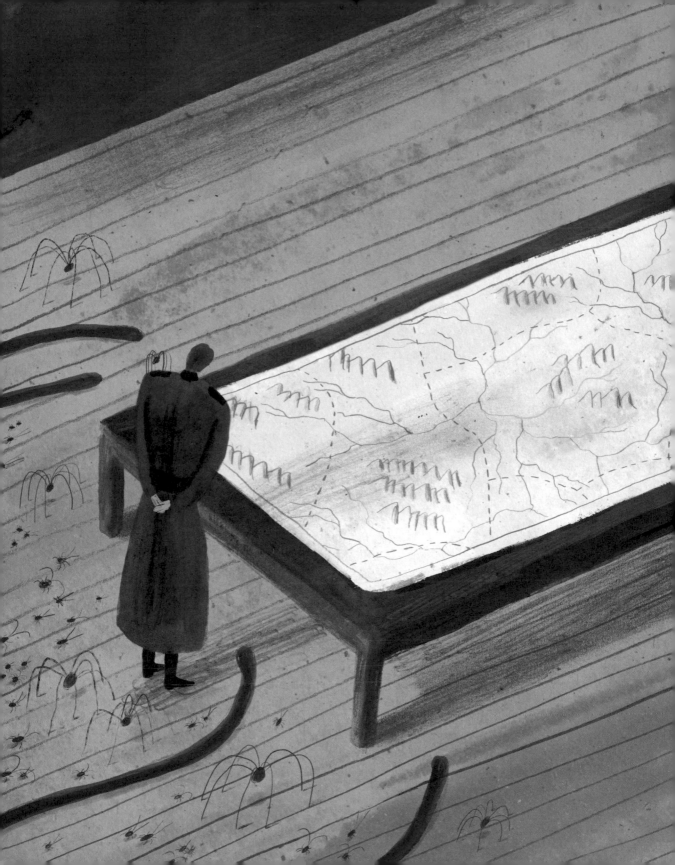

WAR FEEDS ON HATE, AMBITION, AND SPITE.

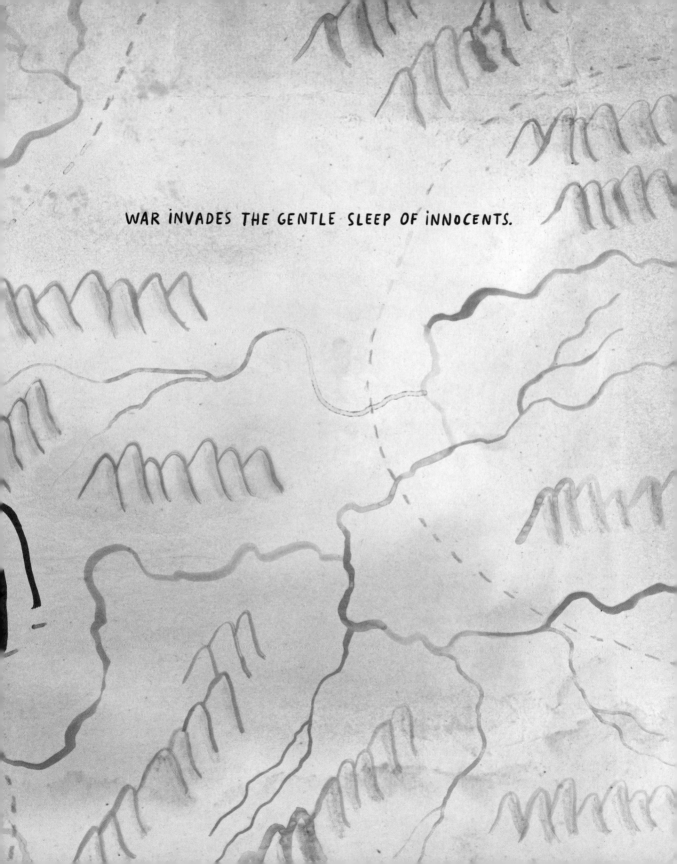

WAR INVADES THE GENTLE SLEEP OF INNOCENTS.

WAR TAKES ON THE FACE OF THE SICKNESS IT BRINGS US.

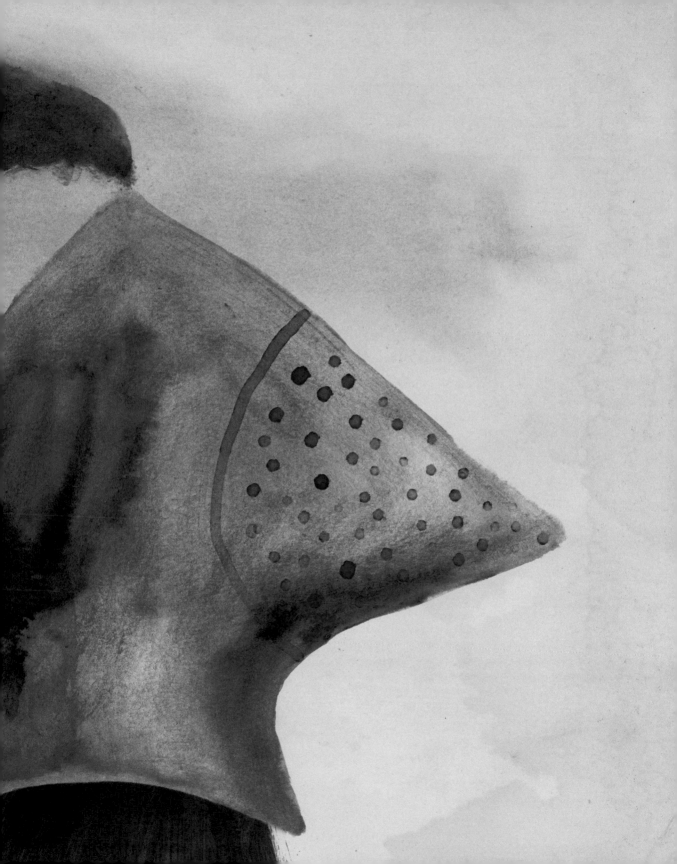

WAR WAS NEVER ABLE TO TELL STORIES.

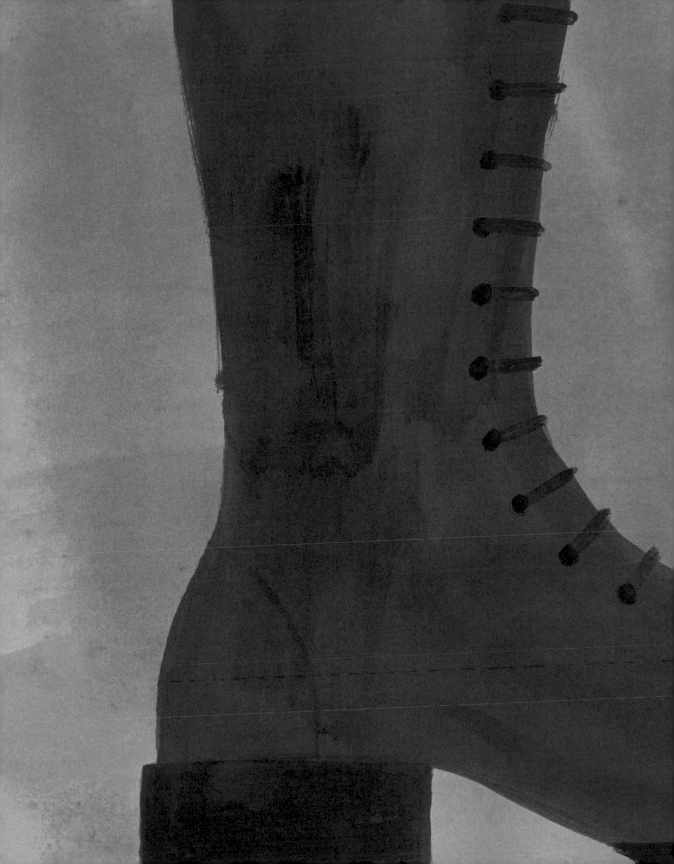

WAR SADDENS, CRUSHES, AND SILENCES.

WAR IS A MACHINE FOR PAIN—
THE EVIL FACTORY OF ALL KINDS OF RAGE.

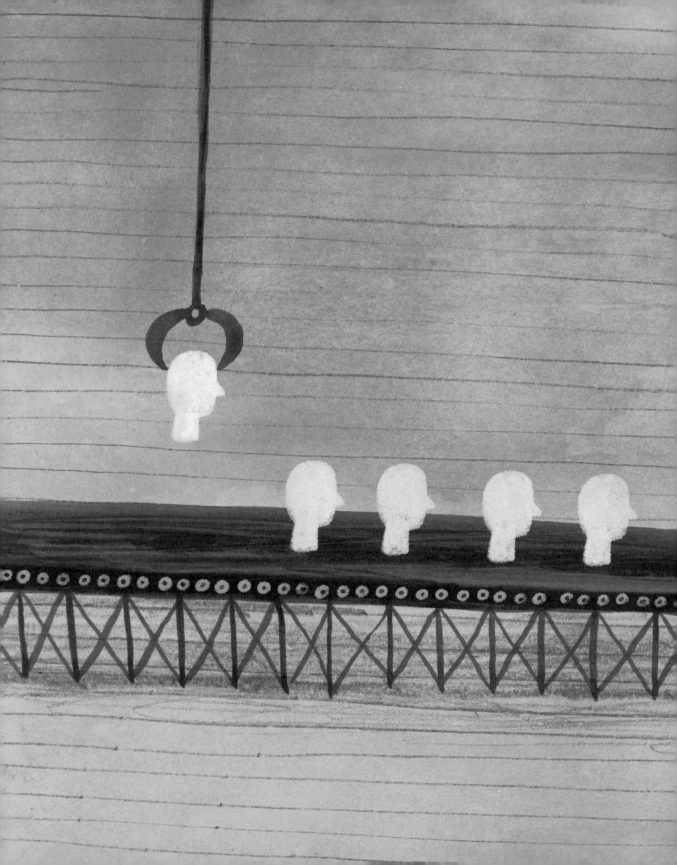

WAR BEGETS SHADOWY, iRON CHILDREN.

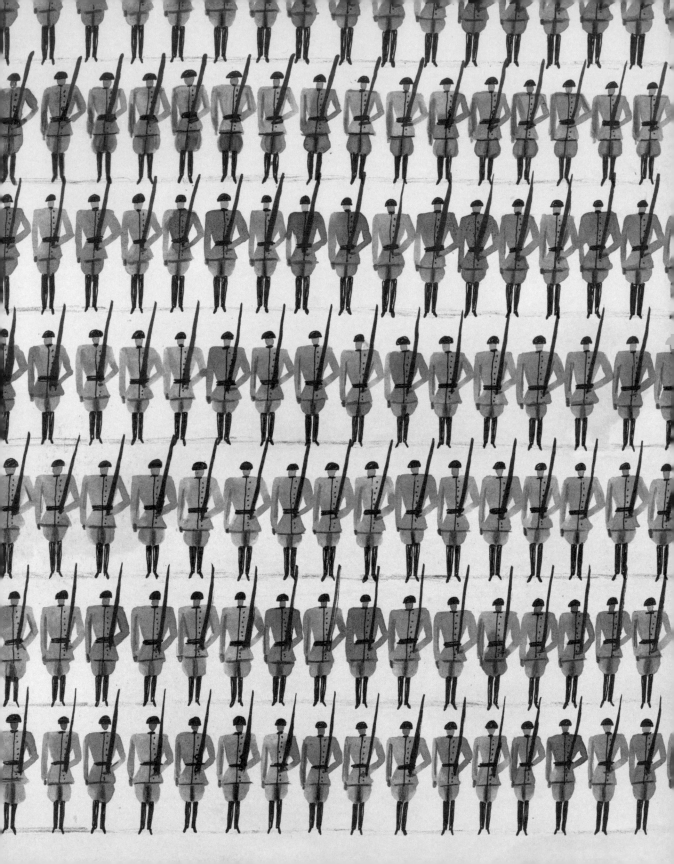

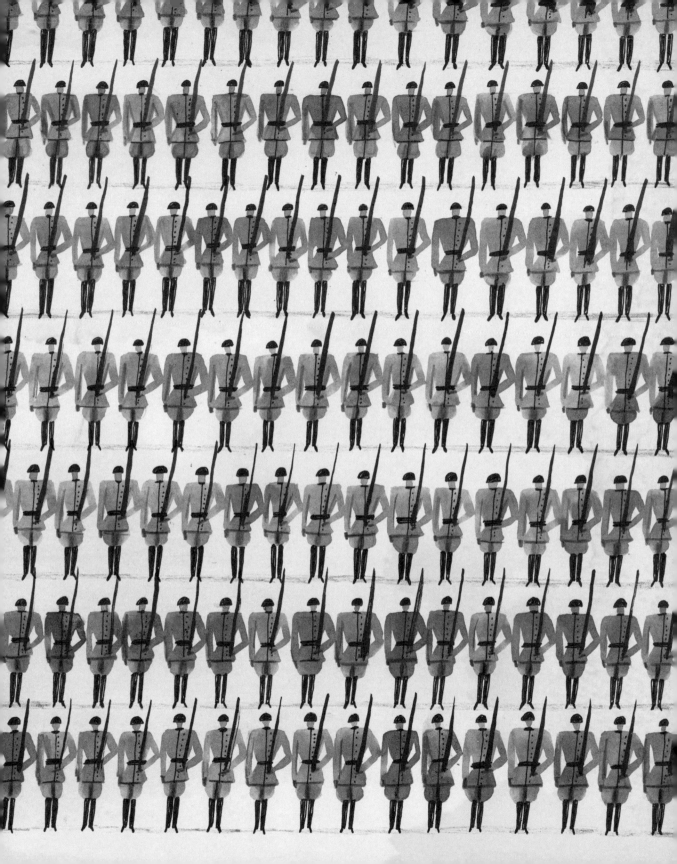

WAR HAS DREAMS OF GLORY THAT WILL BURN EVERYTHING.

WAR IS THE EXACT DESTINATION OF ALL OUR MISERIES.

WAR LIKES TO RULE OVER RUINS.

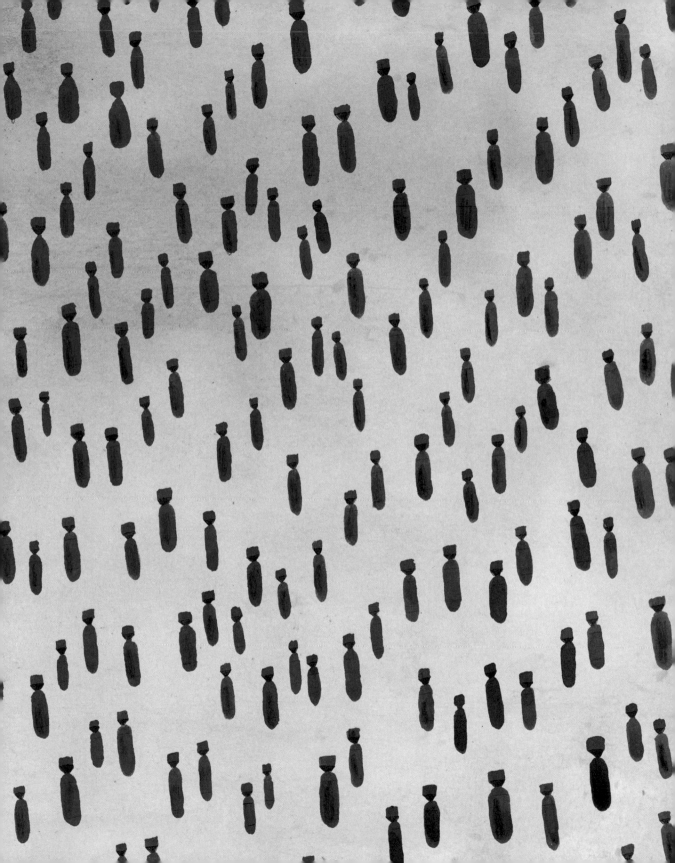

WAR IS DEATH'S FINAL HIDING PLACE.

WAR IS THUNDER AND CHAOS.

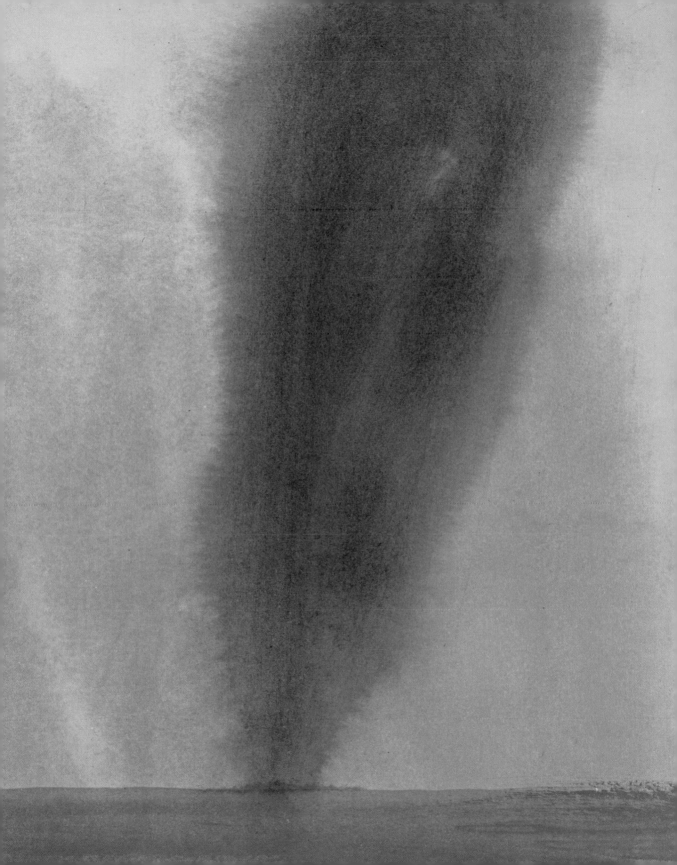

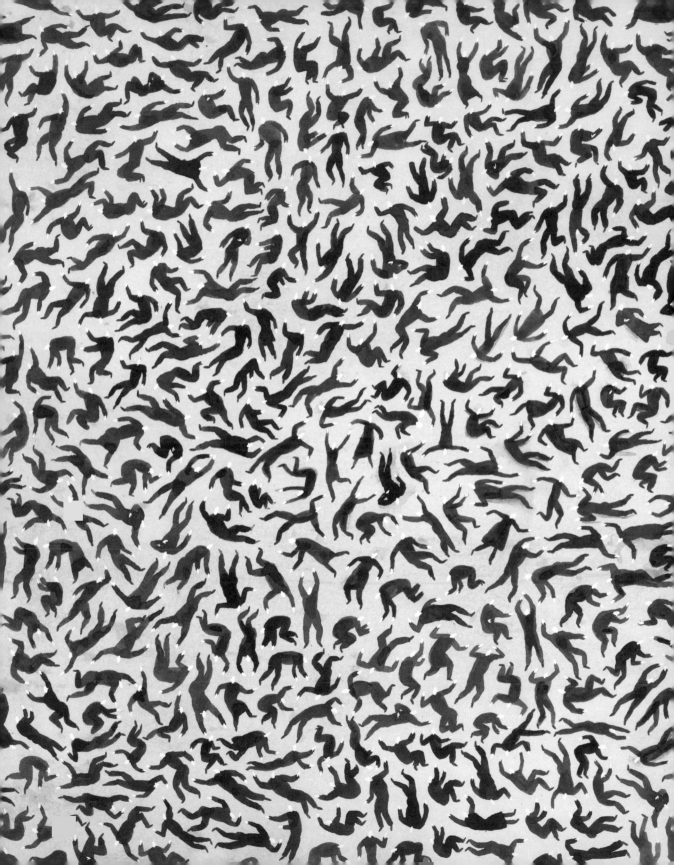

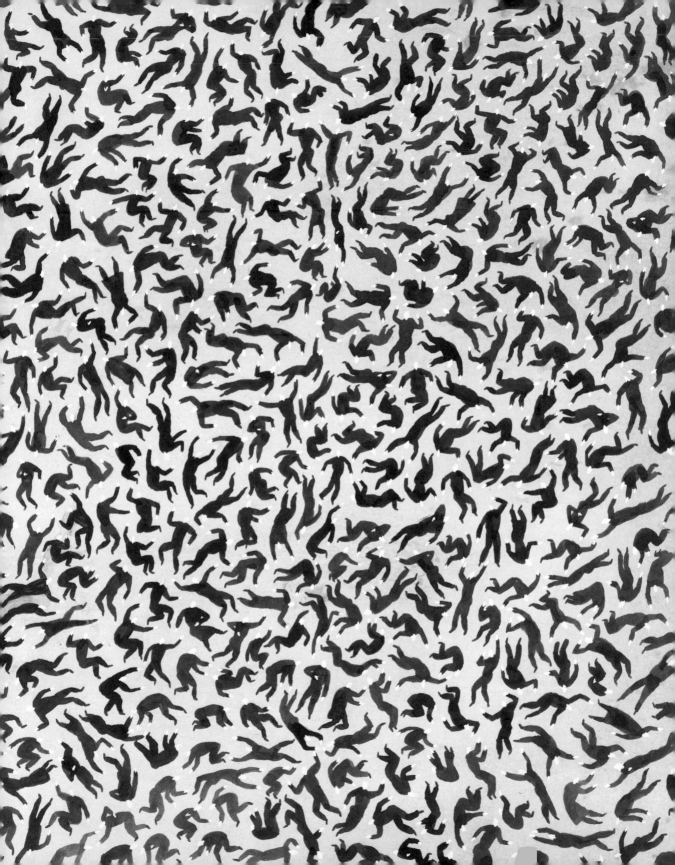

WAR IS SILENCE.

ORIGINALLY PUBLISHED IN PORTUGAL IN 2018 AS A GUERRA
ORIGINAL EDITION COPYRIGHT © 2018 BY PATO LÓGICO EDIÇÕES, LDA.
PORTUGUESE TEXT COPYRIGHT © 2018 BY JOSÉ JORGE LETRIA
ILLUSTRATIONS COPYRIGHT © 2018 BY ANDRÉ LETRIA
ENGLISH TRANSLATION COPYRIGHT © 2021 BY ELISA AMADO
FIRST PUBLISHED IN CANADA, THE U.S., AND THE U.K. BY GREYSTONE BOOKS IN 2021

21 22 23 24 25   5 4 3 2 1

GREYSTONE KIDS / GREYSTONE BOOKS LTD.
GREYSTONEBOOKS.COM

AN ALDANA LIBROS BOOK

CATALOGUING DATA AVAILABLE FROM LIBRARY AND ARCHIVES CANADA
ISBN 978-1-77164-726-7 (CLOTH)
ISBN 978-1-77164-727-4 (EPUB)

MIX
Paper from
responsible sources
FSC® C016973

COPY EDITING BY LINDA PRUESSEN
PROOFREADING BY ELIZABETH MCLEAN
JACKET ILLUSTRATION BY ANDRÉ LETRIA

PRINTED AND BOUND IN CHINA ON ANCIENT-FOREST-FRIENDLY PAPER
BY 1010 PRINTING INTERNATIONAL LTD.

GREYSTONE BOOKS GRATEFULLY ACKNOWLEDGES THE MUSQUEAM,
SQUAMISH, AND TSLEIL-WAUTUTH PEOPLES ON WHOSE LAND
OUR OFFICE IS LOCATED.

GREYSTONE BOOKS THANKS THE CANADA COUNCIL FOR THE ARTS,
THE BRITISH COLUMBIA ARTS COUNCIL, THE PROVINCE OF BRITISH COLUMBIA
THROUGH THE BOOK PUBLISHING TAX CREDIT,
AND THE GOVERNMENT OF CANADA FOR SUPPORTING
OUR PUBLISHING ACTIVITIES.

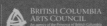